Attack of the Pandroid!

Written & Illustrated by
Gregg Schigiel

HATTER
entertainment

Editor: Polly Watson
Cover illustration and design: Gregg Schigiel
Book design: Gregg Schigiel

Thanks: Jerzy Drozd, Chris Giarrusso, Dave
Giarrusso, David Halvorson, Rob Lemon, Mark
Mariano, Catherine Tutrone

TABLE OF CONTENTS

CHAPTER ONE

Space Sharks and Cosmic Barks

Wonderbear, the Earth's most powerful zooperhero, flew several thousand miles away from Earth, into space. There he joined a few members of the Cosmic Collar Corps, a galactic squad of dogs who policed the galaxy using powers granted by their cosmic collars. And right now all of them were facing down a nasty shiver of giant Neptunian space sharks!

The giant sharks gnashed their rows of sharp teeth at the heroes. The Corps used their cosmic collars to create protective force fields and to fire cosmic blasts at the alien sharks. Meanwhile, Wonderbear kept his distance and used his laser eyes to fight off the massive menacing jaws. Even though he was mostly invincible, it would still hurt him plenty to get bit by a Neptunian space shark.

"Wonderbear, get down!" yelled the Collared Spaniel, leader of the Cosmic Collar Corps. The largest of the giant space sharks was coming toward Wonderbear from behind.

Wonderbear lowered his head and shoulders and the Spaniel fired a bolt of cosmic energy at the giant shark. That only slowed it down. But it was enough to give Wonderbear an opening. He moved quickly so that he was under the attacking shark. Then he flew up like a missile, using the weight and power of his entire body to deliver a fierce, forceful uppercut!

Seeing the power they were up against, the space sharks turned tail and the shiver scattered away.

"Yeah, go back to Neptune, you big ol' toothy terrors!," hooted the Collared Terrier. He liked to think of himself as the Spaniel's equal partner. He was more like her second-in-command.

The Collared Spaniel didn't like that kind of talk. "Come on, Terrier," she said. "No need to add insult to injury. Besides, we're trying to teach our new recruit how to be a hero, remember?" She pointed a paw at the newest member of the Cosmic Collar Corps, Cadet Frenchie.

Frenchie, meanwhile, wasn't paying much attention to them. She was staring wide-eyed at Wonderbear. Everyone in the world knew about Wonderbear and here he was, in the fur.

"Thanks for joining us, Wonderbear," said the Collared Spaniel. "It's good for our new recruit to see Earth's greatest zooperhero in action."

"Well, Spaniel, you know I'm always happy to help. I know you'd do the same for us down on Earth," replied Wonderbear. He looked at the admiring youngster. "Though I don't often work with children. I'm usually saving them. Zooperhero work can get pretty dangerous, young pup."

Terrier joked, "Hey Spaniel, I think we gotta train the cadet in how to interact with other zoops, huh?"

"Heh, heh. I think so," Spaniel replied, adding, "Though she kinda reminds me of you when you first met War Horse."

While Wonderbear was the most powerful zooperhero on Earth and loved the world over, War Horse was the most respected zooperhero.

Terrier blushed under his mask.

"Hey," said Wonderbear though a wide grin, "even I was starstruck meeting War Horse, Spaniel."

Terrier smiled. Even by just saying something supportive like that, Wonderbear was behaving heroically.

"Yeah, me too," admitted the Collared Spaniel.

"I might meet War Horse?" asked Cadet Frenchie, now even more starstruck. "Um, no offense, Wonderbear, you're like, super awesome."

They all chuckled.

Suddenly, the Collared Spaniel put a paw to one of her ears attentively. She was getting a report from the Cosmic Collar Corps' galactic satellite base.

"All right canines," she said, changing her fun and friendly tone to one of command and authority. "Seems our radar team has noted more of those energy fluxes and disturbances in the deepest reaches of the galaxy. It's time to get moving."

"Disturbances?" asked Wonderbear.

"For now we don't know much," explained Spaniel. "It could just be a series of solar flares in another galaxy or interdimensional static. I'm sure it's nothing we haven't handled before."

"Stop that, Terrier," scolded Spaniel. "Let's not tell scary campfire stories. Let's go."

"Thanks again, Wonderbear," said Spaniel.

"Of course. Let me know if I can help in any way," he said.

Collared Spaniel tapped a panel on one of her wristbands and opened a hyperspace portal. She, Terrier, and Frenchie flew into it and zapped away. Wonderbear floated in the quiet of space before heading back to Earth.

As he soared in the silence he looked around and thought. He thought about how he himself came to Earth as a cub alone aboard a small hibernation pod. He thought about how to this day he doesn't know the truth about where he's from.

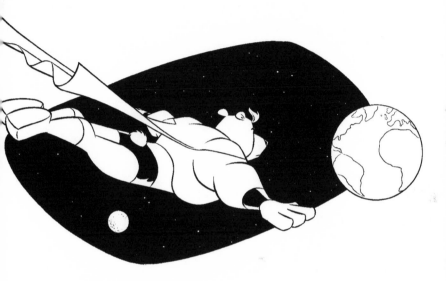

Was he an alien from another planet?

Was he an Earth bear who as a baby had been granted his powers by an alien race?

Had he been born in space, on an Earth space station where experiments were being conducted, only to get sent to Earth before that space station mysteriously vanished?

Of course, in the end it doesn't matter where he was born or how he got his powers. Wonderbear was raised on Earth. His adopted parents taught him how to control his powers. And more than that, they taught him right from wrong. Earth is the only home he knows, and he proudly uses his incredible powers to protect it and all the animals that live there.

CHAPTER TWO

The Secret Labs of Dr. Len Locke

Back on Earth, in Alpha City, stands the tall office building tower of Locke Labs and Logistics, also known as LL&L or L3. The L3 building is one of the tallest skyscrapers in the city. And LL&L are known throughout the world for their technical innovations in everything from refrigerators and toilets to medicines and surgical tools. There are rumors that LL&L works with many countries around the world developing weapons systems.

But fame and rumors aside, there's something about the L3 tower no animal talks about. It's something hardly any animals know about.

Under the parking garage and the lower-level basement labs and research rooms, there are more levels. Those sub-basements house a super-secret bunker base.

In that secret space, Dr. Leonard "Len" Locke watched Wonderbear reenter the Earth's atmosphere on several monitors. He knit his brow tightly in anger.

Dr. Leonard Locke was once a brilliant and promising young scientist. He had ideas that could help solve many of the world's problems. And while he used his genius to invent and develop many useful and helpful things, that wasn't his true aim.

Dr. Locke didn't think things like disease and hunger and climate change were the important challenges facing the planet. He was convinced the biggest and most menacing problem the world faced was

Wonderbear. Dr. Locke thought the mysteries of Wonderbear's origins hid dark and dangerous secrets that could spell disaster for the Earth. Locke became obsessed in his belief that the most powerful zooperhero on Earth was actually the planet's greatest threat.

The way Dr. Locke put it, "If I had that kind of power, I could rule the world!"

And so, Dr. Locke thought that's what Wonderbear would eventually do - take over the world. Thus the doctor had tried many times to use his genius to destroy Wonderbear.

One of Locke's earliest efforts involved trying to give himself Wonderbear-like powers. Dr. Locke created a formula he was convinced would work. He was so sure of it that he performed no tests of any kind. He didn't want to give anyone else the powers. But the formula did not work at all as he expected. He got zero superpowers. Instead, the potion turned his skin and feathers the color of gold, and even worse, made him more insane than he was before.

"Here he comes," sneered Locke, out loud to no one but himself. "The beloved 'hero' returns to Earth. I can already hear him telling everyone he stopped an invading alien force. But I can see through his lies. It wouldn't surprise me to discover he's working with the Neptunians! I'll bet he used those collared canines to cover his tracks and make it look like some space battle. But clearly he's forming a secret interplanetary alliance that will eventually lead to him conquering the Earth once and for all…"

He rose from his seat and left the monitor room, walking down a dimly lit hallway as he continued talking to himself.

"…which I am certain has been his ultimate goal since he arrived on our planet as a baby—if that's even true. We know nothing about where he's from. And sadly, none of my fellow animals have the intellect I do that would allow them to see him for what he really is."

He approached a door farther down the corridor and tapped a long code on a number pad on the wall to open it.

"Of course they don't. None of them have the nth-level brainpower that I do. While those fools blindly heap love and praise on that…bear…in due time they'll have me, Dr. Leonard Locke to thank. For I am the only animal on this planet working to truly save it."

Dr. Locke entered a room brimming with technology. On one wall were more monitors, still showing images of Wonderbear. On another were lights and switches, dials and buttons and levers. The room hummed and beeped and blipped and pinged. All kinds of cables and wires led from the ceiling to the center of the room, where they attached to a very large capsule shaped coffin-like enclosure.

Dr. Locke put his hand on the capsule. It was filled with a cloudy mist and a large form. Someone, or *something*, was inside.

"And when I release this, my latest creation," the mad vulture cackled, "the threat of Wonderbear will be ended once and for all. Bwahahahah!"

CHAPTER THREE

Black and White and Robotic All Over

Above Dr. Locke's secret underground base, on the streets of the city, no one could hear his maniacal laugh. Alpha City was full of Saturday hustle and bustle, with animals going about their usual routines.

A rhinoceros police officer was giving an ostrich a parking ticket. A pack of business wolves ate lunch at an outdoor cafe. A tortoise and moose walked into a museum. No one had a clue what was happening just a few hundred feet below them.

Among the animals going about their daily lives was a young elephant, ten-year-old Shira Jaffrey. Shira was out with her mother at a shopping center just twenty miles away from L3 Tower.

Shira's mother was on the phone and Shira was bored. It was no fun standing around listening to one side of a grown-up conversation about forms or something equally dull. It was extra torture because at that moment they were standing outside one of her favorite stores, Wendy's Wonders, a toy and costume shop. Not knowing how long her mom would be on the phone, Shira mimed to ask her mother if she could go in.

Her mother didn't like being interrupted. But she put a hand over the phone's microphone, "Fine, but I'll be in to get you as soon as I'm off this call," she said.

Shira hopped up and down with excitement. Her mother added, "And we're not buying anything. You have enough costumes at home already."

Her mom was right. She had a lot of outfits at home. Shira loved to play dress-up and make up characters and put on shows. But even with the no-buying rule in place, Shira excitedly scuttled into the store. She suddenly hoped her mom's boring adult call would go very, very long.

Inside the store she went directly to the costume section. Just because she couldn't buy anything didn't mean she didn't want to see what might be new, for next time, when maybe she would be allowed to buy something.

She was looking at some silly hats when--

The store around her shook. Toys and costumes

rattled and fell off their shelves and racks. "Is it an earthquake?" she wondered, as she ran to the front door to get to her mother.

But she couldn't get to her mother. The door was blocked by fallen debris and a collapsed beam. Shira only saw smoke and dust and shadows of bodies moving around.

"Everyone, follow me out the back door," yelled Wendy, the store owner. Customers ran to the back. Shira worried about her mother...and knew her mother was worrying about her.

•••

Out in the front of the store a massive cloud of dust and smoke filled the air. Animals who had been going peacefully about their day were now confused and scared. And, as Shira imagined, her mother was worried about her child, seemingly trapped inside Wendy's Wonders.

While she tried to make her way to the store, blocked by the fallen beam, a red light appeared in the smoky cloud. And as the dust settled the shoppers saw something that chilled them all to the bone.

"What is that?!" screamed a petrified porcupine.

"I-I-Is that a…bear?" stuttered a frightened fox.

"I think it's a robot," offered a stunned stork.

"Whatever it is," said the porcupine, "I don't think it's a zooperhero."

All three of them were right. Standing before them was a part-panda, part-robot…a monstrous Pandroid!

The strange and sensational Pandroid started to move, lumbering along its destructive path. It wasn't entering any stores to steal money or items from them. It wasn't attacking any specific animals. It didn't seem to have a target at all. It was just destroying for destruction's sake. No one could make any sense of it. And that uncertainty only made everyone more scared.

Some security guards charged at it. Pandroid swatted them away like someone might wipe crumbs from a table.

The scared animals wondered what could possibly stop this beast's rampage.

"Stop right there, creature!" came a familiar confident and comforting voice from above. Everyone looked up to see Wonderbear hovering over the Pandroid.

"My daughter!" yelled Shira's mother toward the hero. "I can't find my daughter!"

Wonderbear turned his attention to her, "Ma'am, don't worry, I'll look for--"

Wonderbear was struck by Pandroid, who had rocketed up toward him, delivering a powerful punch that sent Wonderbear reeling.

Pandroid could fly! Pandroid was strong!

As Wonderbear spun from the unexpected blow, he wondered "Just what in the heck am I up against?"

CHAPTER FOUR

Pachyderm Punch

Pandroid packed serious power. He was much faster than he looked. And the cyber-bear had something else about him, too.

Something was making it very hard for Wonderbear to defend himself. It wasn't that Wonderbear's powers weren't working. He could still punch with super strength, fly with wondrous speed, and fire beams of energy from his eyes. But his senses were off. He could see and hear and smell better than most any animal on the planet. Except now…

Wonderbear was downright disoriented. He had very few known weaknesses. Could this creature know about one that Wonderbear didn't even know he had?

Wonderbear started to worry. What if he couldn't defeat Pandroid? What would happen to the innocent animals below? He thought about the mother elephant looking for her daughter and how badly he wanted to help her.

But Wonderbear didn't have time to worry. Pandroid flew toward him, robot arm pulled back to throw another punch. But before that punch came, Wonderbear spied a pink and gray blur from the corner of his eye.

Something sent Pandroid flying off. That something was a pink-costumed elephant zooperhero with a big smile and even bigger energy.

"Hiya, Wonderbear! I'm uh, um…Elephantasica? Yeah Elephantastica!" said the newly arrived hero energetically. "I'm here to help!"

Elephantastica looked over her shoulder to see where Pandroid was. She had really sent him soaring and figured she had another minute or so before he returned.

"I'm gonna be right back, Wonderbear, okay?" She said, as she rocketed down to the streets below before Wonderbear could respond.

Wonderbear couldn't tell if this was more of him being off his senses or what, but he liked having a moment to get his bearings.

Meanwhile, Elephantastica flew down to the wreckage of the shopping center below. She found Shira's mother, who was trying but failing to move the beam blocking the toy store door. The heroic elephant landed next to the worried mother and put a hand gently on her back.

"Mrs. Jaffrey," she said, "Shira sent me to tell you she's okay. There was a back door to the store and everyone got out that way. Your daughter is safe. You don't have to worry about her."

Shira's mother's tears of panic turned to tears of joy. She thanked Elephantastica over and over again, even giving her a great big hug.

"You've very welcome…and you're a really great hugger, but I need to go help Wonderbear," said Elephantastica.

"Oh, of course, yes, thank you, thank you, thank you," Shira's mother said, continuing to thank her new favorite zooperhero. "Now, where is—"

WHOOOSH!!!!

Before Mrs. Jaffrey could finish her question, Elephantastica launched back into the sky. She returned to the scene of the battle just in time to see Wonderbear fire his eye blasts at Pandroid.

The blast hit Pandroid in his non-robot shoulder. Pandroid's body reacted, but it was creepy how he never said anything, didn't even utter a sound of pain.

"Nice shot, Wonderbear!" Elephantastica cheered, as she flew at Pandroid from behind. She wanted to get him in some kind of hold to stop him. She ended up getting a grip on his head. Pandroid reacted quickly, using his powerful robot legs to kick back, hitting her in the stomach and sending her crashing into a nearby building. Her grasp was pretty tight, though, and she tore off Pandroid's robot ear as she went flying.

Pandroid, with sparks crackling from his missing ear hole, turned to Wonderbear. The brave bear was flying toward him. Pandroid's robot eye glowed with power before releasing a powerful dark-energy blast at the oncoming hero. Wonderbear was starting to feel his senses return to full strength, but it was too little too late. He was hit!

With both heroes momentarily stunned, the battle-damaged Pandroid made his escape from the scene.

•••

Wonderbear recovered quickly and saw that Pandroid was missing. He checked on Elephantastica.

"Are you okay, Elephantastica?" he asked.

"Yeah," she said, smiling wide, "That hurt, but I've had worse ouchies. I once cut my finger real bad."

Wonderbear wondered if he'd heard that right. He was worried she'd maybe hit her head on the building harder than she realized.

"You might want to take some more time to recover," he suggested. "I know from experience how powerful that…thing is. I just wish I knew where it came from… or how it's been able to affect me the way that it has."

"Maybe this will help?" she asked, opening her hand to reveal the piece of Pandroid she'd torn off in her palm.

Wonderbear raised an eyebrow and grinned. "It just night, Elephantastica. And I know exactly the right someone who can help."

CHAPTER FIVE

REPAIRS

Dr. Locke sat in front of one of his walls of monitors in his secret underground headquarters. The capsule coffin behind him was now open and empty. He watched the battle between Pandroid and Wonderbear and Elephantastica. The villainous vulture was very unhappy.

"No! No! No! No!" he yelled in the empty room. "Who is that elephant interloper? Why is she sticking her trunk where it doesn't belong?! I finally had Wonderbear outmatched. He would have lost if not for that party-crashing pachyderm!"

A light on his giant computer console blinked on. Dr. Locke pushed several buttons and flipped some switches. He turned as a large circle on the wall to his left opened. The opened wall revealed a tunnel that turned upward. A gust of wind came rushing from the tunnel, ruffling Dr. Locke's golden feathers. This was followed by a loud BOOM, as Pandroid landed at the base of the tunnel with force.

The creature lumbered down the tunnel toward Dr. Locke. The robot part of his head sparked where his ear piece was torn off. Smoke trailed from other damaged robot parts. Some of the fur on his panda arm was missing where he'd been hit by Wonderbear's eye blast. A wound showed on the skin underneath.

While Pandroid was more than enough of a challenge for Wonderbear, the appearance of Elephantastica had changed things. Pandroid had used up most of his power supply. He was now very slow and weak. Dr. Locke moved toward the cy-bear and helped lead him to the capsule in the center of the lab.

"While I might be upset you didn't destroy Wonderbear – which is what I created you to do – that elephant was a surprise to us both. And an unwelcome one at that. So I am pleased to have you returned," Locke said, laying Pandroid down inside the coffin-like cylinder. "Because now I can repair the damage done to you. And more importantly, I can make some necessary upgrades and improvements..."

Dr. Leonard Locke laughed a sinister laugh.

•••

At the same time, in neighboring Delta City, Wonderbear and Elephantastica were in an unknown underground location as well: the secret headquarters of the zooperheroes Moonwolf and his young sidekick, Crescent.

Moonwolf was very serious about his zooperhero work. Because of that, many animals and some other zooperheroes thought of him as unfriendly. But Wonderbear knew him better. Moonwolf was a great friend and ally in the fight against evil. Crescent, meanwhile, was twelve years old and full of energy and excitement about being a zooperhero. Moonwolf and Crescent seemed like opposites, but they shared a bond and were a truly excellent and dynamic duo.

Moonwolf was incredibly intelligent. He applied his smarts, and his various scanners and computer equipment, to carefully examine the piece of Pandroid's ear. Wonderbear looked on with great interest.

"There it is," said Moonwolf softly, more to himself than to Wonderbear.

"There what is, Moonwolf? What are you seeing?" Wonderbear asked.

Moonwolf zoomed in on the screen to show small crystals inside the broken robot ear. He explained, "See those crystal shards and how they're set in their metallic chambers? When given a charge, they send out a sound with a very specific tone and pitch. It's a sound most animals can't hear at all. But with your super-senses I'm thinking you can hear it without even realizing it. I believe that is why you were so disoriented in battle."

Moonwolf tested his theory by giving the scrap of metal an electrical jolt. Wonderbear felt his head get "cloudy."

"Whoa…" Wonderbear said through the mental haze, "that's definitely it."

Moonwolf turned off the electric pulse.

"So…" said Wonderbear, feeling better, "…this Pandroid tried to use my own super abilities against me. But why? Where did Pandroid come from?"

"I might be able to figure that out, too," said Moonwolf.

Wonderbear waited attentively. Meanwhile, Elephantastica's attention was somewhere else. Crescent was showing Elephantastica some of their gear.

Crescent showed their grappling hooks, smoke bombs, wall-grippers, rebreathers, ultraviolet spectrum goggles, and more. She showed Elephantastica their car, motorcycles, and jetpacks. And she showed her their different costume options. Costumes for icy-cold adventures and for desert missions. There was underwater gear for a team-up with the aquatic hero Watermane, and even space suits.

"Wow," said Elephantastica. "All that stuff is amazing. All those different supersuits are mega-awesome. They make me want to have different costumes myself."

"Well, I usually just wear this one I have on," said Crescent. "I mean, we've used those other ones maybe once each? And honestly, we've never even been to space, so like, we've never actually worn the space suits. The Cosmic Collar Corps tend to handle that stuff anyway."

"Yeah, that makes sense," said Elephantastica, before asking a question she couldn't get out of her head. "So you don't have any powers? And you're a kid hero, like

I— I um, uh, am impressed!"

"Oh, we have powers, Moonwolf and me," explained
Crescent. "I'm stronger and faster than a regular wolf.
I have better eyesight and smell, too, especially during
a crescent moon. And Moonwolf's powers are at their
peak during a full moon, so like, we've got all the bases
covered, ha ha!"

"That's so cool," exclaimed Elephantastica. "Do you,
like, go to school? Have you ever met another kid
zooperhero? Do your parents know you're a zooperhero?
Wait, is Moonwolf your dad?"

Crescent looked at Elephantastica with an uneasy
expression. Elephantastica caught herself.

"Oh no," said Elephantastica. "Wait, secret identities of course, I'm sorry for being so nosy. My mom says I ask too many questions. My dad says it's a good quality. I'm talking too much, I know."

"It's okay. Moonwolf says I can be kinda high-energy and overeager, too," said Crescent. "Speaking of, let's see what they're doing over there."

They joined Moonwolf and Wonderbear. Moonwolf was explaining what he had figured out.

"Based on a fur sample I was able to pull from you, Wonderbear, the fur matches that of a panda named Arnold Chen. Corporal Chen was a soldier who was very badly injured during his last mission. He was sent for treatment to a special hospital. But according to all records I could find, he did not survive."

Name: Arnold Chen
Rank: Colonel
Status: Deceased

Colonel Arnold Chen's ...ere too severe ...atient was lost. ...en's body was ... to a secondary facility. The location of ...own, ...nfi- ...l re-

"Hm," said Wonderbear, "That's terrible."

Moonwolf continued, "That's what we know of the panda part of Pandroid. For the robot side, based on these mechanical parts…the metals and fittings are very specific. They are exclusively used by one company. And it's the same company that ran the special hospital that was supposed to treat Corporal Chen."

"What company is it?" asked Elephantastica, totally caught up in Moonwolf's explanation.

"Locke Labs and Logistics," answered Moonwolf.

"Goldie!" Wonderbear exclaimed, punching one paw into another, "I should have known it'd be him."

"'Goldie'?" asked Elephantastica?

Crescent explained, "The head of LL&L, Dr. Leonard Locke. Everyone thinks he's a brilliant scientist and inventor. He's more of a mad scientist, though. He tried to give himself powers and now he's all gold, like, in color. He's not made of gold. But we call him 'Goldie.'"

"Is that his power?" asked Elephantastica.

'Oh no. That's what happened instead of him getting powers," clarified Crescent, adding, "Oh, and he totally hates Wonderbear."

"What?" Elephantastica couldn't believe it. "Why?!"

"He's convinced I'm his enemy and a threat to the planet," answered Wonderbear. "He's done all kinds of dangerous and deadly things trying to get to me. That he's somehow connected to Pandroid is not good. I'm afraid to think of how Pandroid came to be...or what I can do to stop him."

Moonwolf chimed in, "I have something that will help disable the effect of the crystals. But if he's as powerful as you say, I don't know if that alone will be enough to defeat him."

CHAPTER SIX

Panda-monium!

"Maybe then the best plan is to take this fight directly to Goldie's door," said Wonderbear.

He was fired up. He couldn't help but think of all the destruction and fear caused by Pandroid. He hated thinking about Arnold Chen being used for such a thing. And of course he thought about how all of it was because of Dr. Leonard "Goldie" Locke.

"You know you can't do that, my friend," Moonwolf said with some sadness. "We might know who Dr. Leonard Locke really is. We know the evil he's done. And I want to see him stopped as badly as you do. But this city, the world, doesn't know that side of him."

Wonderbear let out an annoyed puff from his nostrils.

"They see him as a well-respected citizen," continued Moonwolf. "As far as the world knows, he researches and creates new medicines and treatments. He invents and develops new technologies that make animals' lives easier and fun. If you openly attack Locke or tear through the L3 Tower…that only gives him a chance to convince the world that you are what he thinks you are."

Wonderbear growled in frustration. He knew Moonwolf was right.

•••

After they said their goodbyes, Wonderbear and

Elephantastica were back in the air flying toward Alpha City. It was a very quiet flight.

"So…now what?" asked Elephantastica. The silence was too much for her.

"I'm going to try to find and put a stop to Pandroid, and hopefully to Locke after that," replied Wonderbear.

"Um…I can help," offered Elephantastica. "Like, it's kinda cool how Crescent and Moonwolf are a team, right?"

"They…have their reasons for their partnership. I consider Moonwolf a friend, but I think it's irresponsible of him to let Crescent join him as a zooperhero. It's much too risky a thing for such a young animal to do," said Wonderbear.

Elephantastica was surprised by Wonderbear's answer. She tried to defend Crescent, "Oh, but...she has powers of her own. She's not just an ordinary cub."

"Even so. It's too dangerous for kids to--" Wonderbear stopped talking mid-sentence. He saw Pandroid flying toward them and moving fast.

While they'd been with Moonwolf and Crescent, Dr. Locke had made some repairs and improvements to Pandroid's machine parts.

"Speaking of dangerous," said Wonderbear, as he placed small pods in his ears, "I hope these devices Moonwolf designed to protect me from Pandroid's confusion crystals work..."

"Well, uh, I'm here, too," said Elephantastica, suddenly much more nervous.

Pandroid attacked! He was tougher and more dangerous. But this time Wonderbear was fully able to defend himself and fight back. And Elephantastica was there by his side.

After some fierce fighting, the heroes disabled
Pandroid's weaponry. The monstrous menace was
grounded. He lay quietly on the pavement and seemed
no longer a threat.

The heroes approached Pandroid. With his technology
weakened, they hoped to reach the panda inside.

"Corporal Chen, you're going to be okay," said
Wonderbear. "Whatever was done to you that turned
you into this, we will try to undo."

Pandroid didn't respond. His robot parts sparked, fizzled
and smoked. But he didn't move. His one non-robot eye

stared blankly at nothing, not even blinking.

"Did we damage his hearing?" asked Elephantastica.

"I'm sure he's just in shock," Wonderbear said. He spoke again, slower and louder. "Ar-nold. Chen. I. am. Won-der. bear. This. is. Ele. phan. tas. ti. ca. We. Are. zoo-per- he-roes. We. want. to. help. you."

But Wonderbear and Elephantastica got their own shock. Pandroid moved very suddenly, lurching at them. It swung its panda arm, claws extended. And even more surprising, Pandroid finally spoke.

Elephantastica and Wonderbear leapt back.

Pandroid wasn't just a part robot, part panda. No. It was a part robot, part *zombie* panda!

"I-I-I don't think Arnold Chen is in there, W-w-wonderbear," chattered Elephantastica. "I th-th-hink he's like, a z-z-zombie or something."

"I'm afraid you're too right," agreed Wonderbear, "there's no saving him. Even without the cyborg parts, Pandroid is a threat. We still need to stop him."

Pandroid lunged at Wonderbear. The heroic bear dodged. The techno-monster chomped at him, wildly.

"Don't let it bite you!" hollered Elephantastica, now hovering above the ground. "That's how zombies can turn you into a zombie!" Wonderbear also took to the air to avoid the zombie panda.

Elephantastica continued, "I think I know what we can do."

"You do?" asked Wonderbear, surprised.

"Well, okay," she started to explain, "I think I do.

I'm not like, a zombie expert or anything. But I saw a zombie movie once. Which I totally shouldn't have seen it, because it was way scary and I couldn't fall asleep for like, weeks, and my m--" Elephantastica stopped when she realized she was saying too much.

"Uh, anyway," she resumed, "The way the animals in that movie stopped the zombies was--"

CHOP-CHOP-CHOP-CHOP-CHOP-CHOP

Elephantastica was cut off by the sound of whirring rotors coming from helicopters above them. The heroes flew out of the way as the helicopters came down. They landed several yards from the injured zombie Pandroid.

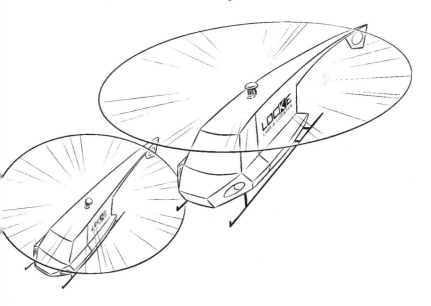

"Locke," muttered Wonderbear through gritted teeth.

Elephantastica said nothing.

The heroes watched as teams of well-equipped, armored animals came out of the high-tech helicopters. From one helicopter, the LL&L crew pulled the tube-coffin from Dr. Locke's secret underground lab base. They brought it over toward Pandroid.

An LL&L agent took a device from their equipment belt and pointed it toward Pandroid. It emitted a beam of light that quickly put the monster to sleep. Several others lifted the heavy body into the capsule, which they then loaded into one of the helicopters.

Meanwhile, a well-spoken gazelle wearing a fancy suit addressed Wonderbear, Elephantastica, and the crowd who had gathered.

"Thank you, Wonderbear and Elephantastica, for your great work in helping subdue this creature. Our city, as always, appreciates all that you do. Locke Labs and Logistics, with our top-rate scientists and technicians, led of course by the brilliant genius Dr. Leonard Locke, will take over from here."

Some reporters on the scene shouted questions over the helicopter's rotors.

"What will you do with that creature?"

"Will you tell us where it came from?

"Is Dr. Locke going to run for mayor?"

"Do you know why it's here?"

"Are zombies real?"

"Is Dr. Locke going to run for president?"

The gazelle answered none of them. She gave no more explanation and boarded the other helicopter. The choppers took flight, headed toward L3 Tower.

Wonderbear's eyes were fixed on them as they became smaller and smaller dots in the sky.

CHAPTER SEVEN

Awkward Goodbyes

Soooo…now what?" wondered Elephantastica, confused.

We should help clean up, assist any animals who need . But beyond that, I think our path ends here," said

Wonderbear. "Goldie is one step ahead of us. Of course he is."

Elephantastica felt helpless. She'd never imagined Wonderbear's words could make her feel that way.

"And I doubt that's the last we'll see of Pandroid...but next time, I'll be more prepared," said Wonderbear, removing the devices from his ears.

"So long as we've learned something, Elephantastica, we haven't lost."

And those words from Wonderbear made her feel more hopeful.

Suddenly, a voice yelled out, "Elephantastica!"

It was Shira's mother, running toward them. "You said my daughter was safe, but...I looked and I couldn't find her behind Wendy's Wonders!"

Before she could respond, Wonderbear stepped in, "You see, Elephantastica...children are a lot of work. To bring one along on a zooperhero adventure, like Moonwolf does, that only makes the job we do that much harder."

"Um, uh, okay," said Elephantastica, now very uneasy and awkward. "Mrs. Jaffrey, wait right here and I'll get your daughter. I know exactly where she is."

Elephantastica flew away.

•••

As she flew, Elephantastica thought about everything Wonderbear had said about Moonwolf and Crescent. Crescent had superpowers and training. And Moonwolf was super smart. He wouldn't have a kid sidekick if that wasn't an intelligent choice. She thought about how she should have brought that up to Wonderbear. Maybe using Moonwolf's smarts would have changed his mind.

She landed in the back alley behind Wendy's Wonders. Shira's mother had been right, there was no one there.

She took another look around, making sure no one was watching, and touched the small earring on her right ear. A bright light appeared a few feet in front of her. The light got larger and turned into a ring. The ring grew larger, revealing a swirl of color inside of it.

Elephantastica leapt into the light ring of swirling color...

…and from the other side of the portal came Shira!

Shira looked back at the swirling colors. She touched the small earring on her right ear. And the magical gateway shrank once again to a single light before it disappeared in a tiny blink.

While she ran back to her mother, Shira again thought about Wonderbear. What would he say if he knew that the hero who'd fought by his side against Pandroid was a ten-year-old girl? Would that be enough to change his mind about kid zooperheroes?

Or, she wondered, if it would make him think she was a liar and a sneak, like Dr. Locke. That would be terrible.

Shira was so distracted by her own thoughts that she bumped into a teenage alligator, who himself was distracted watching Wonderbear fly away from the scene.

"Oh, sorry," they both said.

"Jinx," they both said.

"No problem," they both said.

"Double jinx!" they both said, and laughed.

"Did you see Wonderbear?!" asked the excited alligator. "It would be pretty amazing to meet a zooperhero, don't you think?"

"Yeah," she said, "But even better, imagine being one!"

Shira ran off and found her mother, who of course was thrilled to see her little girl safe and sound.

"I'm so happy you're okay. I was worried sick! But I'm glad you didn't have to see the horrible Pandroid. It was so scary." Shira's mother said. "Oh, I wish Elephantastica was still around so I could tell her how thankful I am."

"Oh, I have a feeling she's very aware," Shira said with a knowing smile.

The End.

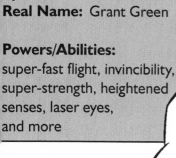

HERO FILE

WONDERBEAR

Species: brown bear
Real Name: Grant Green

Powers/Abilities:
super-fast flight, invincibility,
super-strength, heightened
senses, laser eyes,
and more

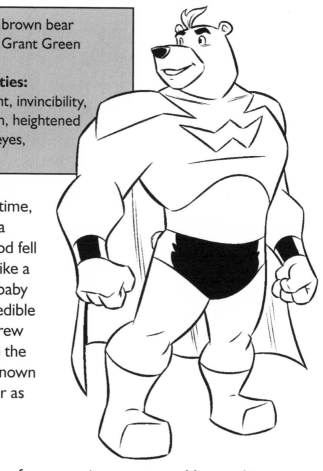

Once upon a time,
a bear cub in a
hibernation pod fell
from the sky like a
meteor. This baby
bear had incredible
powers and grew
up to become the
sooperhero known
he world over as
Wonderbear!

Where he came from remains a mystery. He uses his powers
to help animals here on Earth, the planet he calls home.

When he's not working as a costumed hero, Grant Green is a
voiceover artist for commercials and cartoons.

HERO FILE ELEPHANTASTICA

Species: Asian elephant
Real Name: Shira Jaffrey

Powers/Abilities:
magical flight and super-strength, extra-durability, access to another fantasy dimension

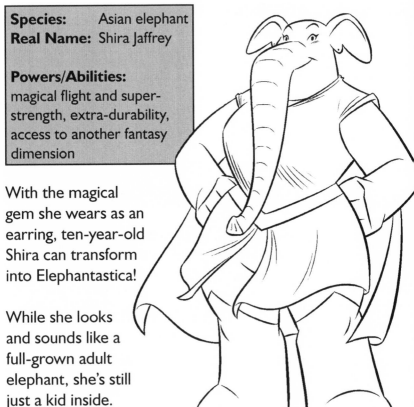

With the magical gem she wears as an earring, ten-year-old Shira can transform into Elephantastica!

While she looks and sounds like a full-grown adult elephant, she's still just a kid inside.

As excited and energetic as she is to be a zooperhero, she worries what might happen if other zooperheroes knew her secret. Not to mention her parents!

She also wonders if she picked the right zooperhero name, sometimes thinking Super Big Girl might be better.

DR. LEONARD LOCKE

Species: vulture
Real Name: Leonard Locke
Nicknames: Len, Goldie

Powers/Abilities:
super-genius intellect in all the sciences - biology, physics, robotics, etc.

Dr. Leonard Locke is a brilliant scientist and inventor. He could use his genius to do so much for the world. But, instead, he focuses his energies on his obsession: Wonderbear.

Locke is convinced the brave bear is a threat to everyone on Earth. But the truth is Locke, because of his madness, is the real danger.

In one of Dr. Locke's earliest schemes, he tried to give himself superpowers like Wonderbear's. His potion didn't work, but it did turn his skin and feathers the color of gold.

Cooperheroes call him "Goldie" because of it. Dr. Locke hates that nickname.

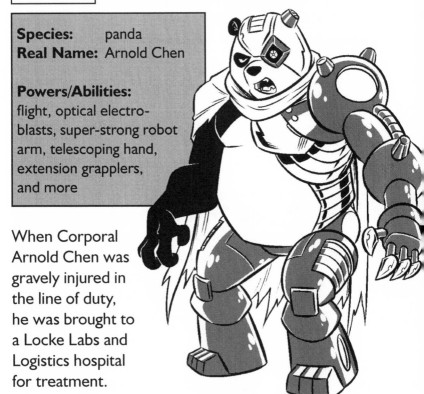

PANDROID

VILLAIN FILE

Species: panda
Real Name: Arnold Chen

Powers/Abilities:
flight, optical electro-blasts, super-strong robot arm, telescoping hand, extension grapplers, and more

When Corporal Arnold Chen was gravely injured in the line of duty, he was brought to a Locke Labs and Logistics hospital for treatment.

All records show that Corporal Chen did not survive. But the truth is that his body was used by Dr. Leonard Locke as the basis for the zombie-panda cyber-bear known as Pandroid.

Pandroid was programmed by Locke to do one thing: destroy Wonderbear. And the mad scientist will continue to upgrade and rebuild Pandroid for that purpose.

ABOUT THE AUTHOR

Gregg Schigiel (Schigiel rhymes with beagle) fell in love with superheroes, animated cartoons, and comic books at an early age. He loved to draw, create characters, and make up stories.

Now, Gregg is the creator, author and illustrator of the *Kids' Comics Award*—winning PIX graphic novel series and of course, ZOOPERHERO UNIVERSE.

In addition, he's drawn for Marvel Comics, DC Comics, Disney, and Nickelodeon, and wrote and drew many stories for SPONGEBOB COMICS.

Gregg has baked prizewinning cookies, enjoys comedy, and makes sure he drinks plenty of water.

GREGG SCHIGIEL

GreggSchigiel.com

ALSO BY GREGG SCHIGIEL

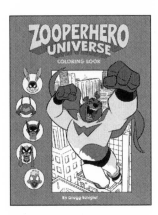

ZOOPERHERO UNIVERSE
Coloring Book

Meet the heroes and villains of
the Zooperhero Universe!
One Hundred pages of dynamic artwork and
compelling character descriptions make this a
coloring book and character guide all in one!

Paperback available
at amazon.com.

PIX
Graphic Novels

Superhero action and
fairy-tale magic meet in
this fun, funny, and thrilling
graphic novel series.

Read free preview chapters
and get your copies at
greggschigiel.com/pix.

UNIQUECORNS Coloring Book

What if animals other than horses were unicorns?
Discover a new world of wildlife—from
swamps to the Sahara, high skies to deep
seas—as they're transformed into the magical
and mythological, awaiting your colors!

Paperback available
at amazon.com.

Made in the USA
Coppell, TX
10 October 2021

63828686R00049